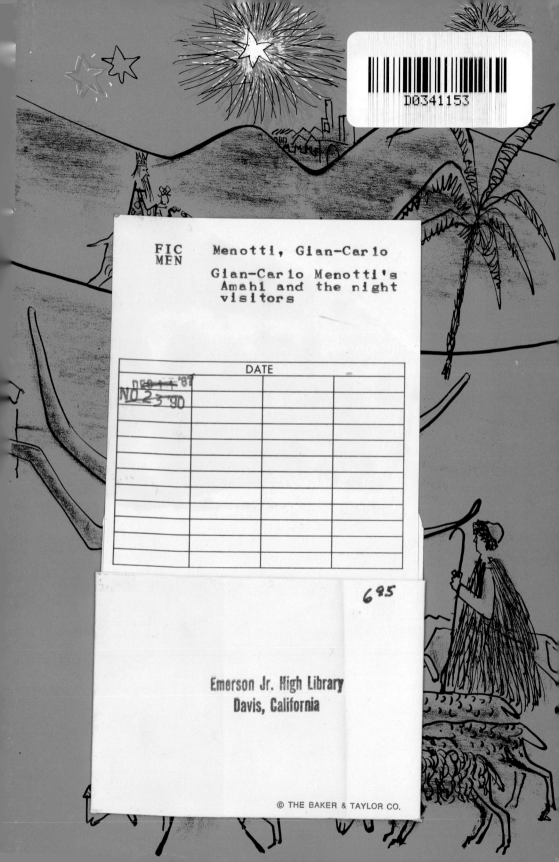

FIC   Menotti, Gian-Carlo
MEN

Gian-Carlo Menotti's
Amahl and the night
visitors

DATE		
DEC 1 1 '87		
NO 23 90		

6 95

Amahl and the Night Visitors

GIAN-CARLO MENOTTI'S

Amahl
and the
Night Visitors

This narrative adaptation by FRANCES FROST
preserves the exact dialogue of the opera

Illustrated by

ROGER DUVOISIN

McGRAW-HILL BOOK COMPANY
New York   Toronto   London

Library of Congress Catalog Card Number: 52-10343

Printed in the United States of America

ISBN 07-41489-0

1920 RABP 7987

Amahl and the Night Visitors

✰ AMAHL ✰
AND
THE NIGHT VISITORS

IT WAS a clear night and cold. Amahl shivered a little under his shepherd's cloak as he sat watching the sky and playing his shepherd's pipe.

Far away he heard the shouts of the other shepherd boys and he longed to play with them. But on the stone beside him lay his crudely made crutch. He could never keep up with them. He must stay here outside his mother's cottage door.

7

Now that his father was dead and his flock of sheep had been sold he had no companions except his thin cat and his little caged sparrow. It saddened him sometimes that these two friends who loved him so well would have nothing to do with each other. Still, they were good company. They liked his music. They always seemed to listen to him so carefully. Inside the cottage they were probably listening now.

He lifted his pipe again and played them a plaintive note. And in the cottage his mother paused in her work to listen too.

This was a strange night, somehow, and Amahl played with a new sense of wonder at the heavens and the constellations beginning to swing up over the hills. In the eastern sky there was a great star that Amahl had never seen before. It had blazed up suddenly with a flaming tail and now it stood steady and bright.

As he watched it, Amahl began to forget his loneliness. It was such a wonderful star.

From the cottage he heard his mother's voice calling him, but he did not answer right away.

"Amahl! Amahl!" she called.

"Oh!" he answered, keeping his eyes on the star.

"Time to go to bed," urged his mother.

8

"Coming!" Amahl shrugged his shoulders under the warmth of the cloak and continued playing. He gazed up at the great star. "Mother, let me stay a little longer."

"The wind is cold," she said anxiously, leaning out of the window.

There had been a light snowfall that day and Amahl knew she was worried for fear he would start sneezing. "But my cloak is warm," he told her. "Let me stay a little longer."

"The night is dark," his mother insisted.

"But the sky is light," Amahl pleaded. "Let me stay a little longer."

"The time is late." She was beginning to sound cross.

Amahl smiled. "But the moon hasn't risen yet. Let me stay a little—"

His mother was really cross this time. She clapped her hands out of the window and warned him,

"There won't be any moon tonight,
but there will be a weeping child very soon,
if he doesn't hurry up and obey his mother."

She pulled the crudely paned window inward with a sharp little bang and Amahl quivered.

9

"Oh, very well." He gave a last look at the great star.

Reluctantly he arose, and tucked his rough crutch under his arm, and hobbled into the cottage. He hung his heavy cloak and shepherd's cap on the pegs at one side of the wooden door and carefully placed his pipe in the far corner where it would be safe. His mother knelt before the low stone fireplace, trying to coax a fire from the few remaining twigs. She looked so thin, kneeling there in her dark-green homespun dress, that Amahl's heart ached.

He was furious at himself because he was a cripple and a boy, instead of a tall strong man like his father who could take care of her. From the bird cage made of twisted vine that hung above his bed, his sparrow twittered at him. He twittered back at her and looked around for his cat. But the cat had gone for a walk.

"What was keeping you outside?" his mother asked, and blew on the twigs.

Amahl returned to the open door and leaned against it. Would she believe him if he told her? He glanced at her doubtfully and gazed back into the night, trying to make up his mind. Then his eagerness to share what he had seen overcame his fear of punishment.

10

He exclaimed,
"Oh, Mother, you should go out and see!
There's never been such a sky!
Damp clouds have shined it
and soft winds have swept it
as if to make it ready for a King's ball.
All its lanterns are lit,
all its torches are burning,
and its dark floor
is shining like crystal.
Hanging over our roof
there is a star as large as a window,
and the star has a tail,
and it moves across the sky
like a chariot on fire."
His mother arose wearily from the feeble fire.
"Oh! Amahl, when will you stop telling lies?
All day long you wander about in a dream.
Here we are with nothing to eat,
not a stick of wood on the fire,
not a drop of oil in the jug,
and all you do is to worry your mother
with fairy tales.
Oh! Amahl, have you forgotten your promise
never, never to lie to your mother again?"

Amahl swung himself away from the door and
cried eagerly,

"Mother darling, I'm not lying.

Please, do believe me."

He followed her across the room and tugged at
her skirt.

"Come outside and let me show you.

See for yourself—see for yourself—"

But she brushed his hand away and crossed the
room to smooth the straw of his pallet. He limped
after her. Impatiently she told him,

"Stop bothering me! Why should I believe you?

You come with a new one every day!

First it was a leopard with a woman's head.

Then it was a tree branch that shrieked and bled.

Then it was a fish as big as a boat,

with whiskers like a cat and wings like a bat

and horns like a goat.

And now it is a star as large as a window—

or was it a carriage?—

And if that weren't enough,

the star has a tail and the tail is of fire!"

Amahl took a deep breath. "But there is a star
and it has a tail this long." He measured the air as
wide as his arms could reach. His mother frowned

and quickly he reduced the size by half. "Well, maybe only—this long. But it's there!"

"Amahl!"

Amahl began to doubt himself a little. In the face of his mother's disbelief, he wondered whether he had really seen the great star or whether it was just another one of his daydreams. He said hesitantly, "Cross my heart and hope to die."

His mother gazed sadly at him, then put her arms about him.

"Poor Amahl!
Hunger has gone to your head.
Dear God, what is a poor widow to do,
when her cupboards and pockets are empty
and everything sold?"

Amahl followed her as she went toward the fire-place. He didn't know how to comfort her. She fixed her own bed of straw and sheepskins on the hard bench and then abruptly sank, weeping, onto the little gray stool by the small flickering fire. He could only stand and stare at her, hating his crutch and his being nothing but a helpless dream-headed boy. His lips began to tremble and he chewed them fiercely.

His mother sobbed,
"Unless we go begging
how shall we live through tomorrow?

My little son, a beggar!"

Amahl limped over to her as fast as he could and kissed her cheek. He stroked her hair tenderly and thought hard.

"Don't cry, Mother dear,
don't worry for me.
If we must go begging,
a good beggar I'll be.
I know sweet tunes to set people dancing.
We'll walk and walk from village to town,
you dressed as a gypsy and I as a clown.
At noon we shall eat roast goose
and sweet almonds,
at night we shall sleep with the sheep
and the stars.
I'll play my pipes, you'll sing and you'll shout.
The windows will open and people lean out.
The King will ride by and hear your loud voice,
and throw us some gold to stop all the noise.
At noon we shall eat roast goose
and sweet almonds,
at night we shall sleep with the sheep
and the stars."

His mother rubbed her face against his rough homespun jacket to wipe away her tears. She stood

up and managed a smile. She bent down to receive his good-night kiss and put her arms around him.

"My dreamer,
You're wasting the light.
Kiss me good night."

When Amahl had kissed her, he limped to his pallet of straw and lay down, placing his crutch carefully beside him. Over his head his caged sparrow fluttered her wings and settled herself for the night. His thin cat came in and tucked herself into the hollow of his arm. Amahl watched his mother fasten the large wooden latch of the door. She took his warm cloak from the peg where he had hung it and spread it over him, tucking him in. She touched his head tenderly, then snuffed out the oil lamp on the mantel. Amahl watched her lie down on the straw and skins on the bench and heard her sigh deeply as she went to sleep.

There was no light in the room now except for the faint glow of the fireplace and the dim radiance of the sky through the thick, crude panes of the window. Amahl turned on his side, shifting the cat, so that he could face toward the sky.

Suddenly he heard the jingle of silvery bells and the sound of strange music far in the distance.

18

He thought drowsily that he was dreaming again. And then he heard three strange voices chanting together through the night. Amahl sat up. His mother was sound asleep. His thin cat slept, her tail over her forepaws and half over her nose. Amahl listened, cocking his head, and this time he thought he heard the silvery bells swaying nearer and heard the three unknown voices chanting together,

"From far away we come and farther must we go.
How far, how far, my crystal star?"

Certainly he was dreaming. He shook his head and lay down again. But once more he heard the voices calling,

"The shepherd dreams inside the fold.
Cold are the sands by the silent sea."

Amahl raised himself on one elbow and listened hard. The voices were coming closer.

"Frozen the incense in our frozen hands,
heavy the gold.
How far, how far, my crystal star?"

Amahl threw back his cloak, seized his crutch, and struggled to his feet. He hobbled to the window, making as little noise as possible so as not to awaken his mother. He gasped as he peered through a pane. Was he still dreaming?

Out of a fold in the hills came a marvelous procession. Three stately camels with gold and silver bridles paced into view, bearing three tall figures, richly dressed. Who could they be? Amahl wanted to call out to his mother but he didn't dare. She would think he was making up stories again and this time she might really spank him. He pressed his nose against the window.

The trappings of the camels glittered in the starlight, and the figures looked like three royal kings. Each of them held something in his hands very carefully. Amahl shut his eyes and pushed his forehead against the pane to make sure he was awake. He opened his eyes and gulped. The mysterious figures were actually coming toward the cottage. He shifted on his crutch and tried another windowpane.

The camel bells jingled and gleamed as the three figures dismounted in Amahl's own yard. Then a fourth figure appeared who walked heavily, bent beneath a load of bundles. This must be the servant. He tied the camels to the fig trees in the yard, after putting his bundles near the door.

Amahl backed away from the window when he saw one of the splendid figures approach the door.

He was dreaming, all right, but it would make a wonderful story to tell the other children, although he knew from sad experience that they wouldn't believe him, any more than his mother had when he had told her about the great star.

As he retreated from the window, he saw the tall figure with the long white beard lift his hand to knock on the wooden door.

At the sound of the knock, Amahl's mother awoke with a start but didn't move from her bed on the bench. "Amahl," she said drowsily, "go and see who's knocking at the door."

"Yes, Mother." He went to the door and opened it a crack, his heart thudding in his chest. He closed the door quickly and rushed to his mother.

"Mother, Mother, Mother, come with me.
I want to be sure that you see what I see."
His mother raised herself on her elbow.
"What is the matter with you now?
What is all this fuss about?
Who is it, then?"

Amahl was shaking with excitement. "Mother—" he stopped. He hardly dared tell her what he had seen. "Outside the door there is"—he swallowed and went on with an effort—"there is a king with a crown."

His mother gazed toward the roof and asked the heavens,

"What shall I do with this boy,
What shall I do?
If you don't learn to tell the truth,
I'll have to spank you!"

There was another knock at the door and she sighed and sank back on the sheepskins. She told Amahl severely,

"Go back and see who it is
and ask what they want."

Amahl hurried to the door and again opened it just a crack and stared. He hobbled back to his mother.

"Mother, Mother, Mother, come with me.
I want to be sure that you see what I see."

His mother shook her head at him and asked,

"What is the matter with you now?
What is all this fuss about?"

Amahl gazed at her desperately.

"Mother—I didn't tell the truth before."

His mother smiled at him.

"That's a good boy."

Amahl gulped hurriedly,

"There is not a king outside."

His mother almost laughed.

"I should say not!"

Amahl blurted,

"There are *two* kings!"

His mother sat up and wailed to the roof again,

"What shall I do with this boy,

what shall I do, what shall I do?

Hurry back and see who it is,

and don't you dare make up tales!"

Amahl rushed to the door once more and rushed back, crying,

"Mother, Mother, Mother, come with me.

If I tell you the truth

I know you won't believe me."

His mother said shortly, "Try it for a change."

"But you won't believe me," Amahl protested.

"I'll believe you if you tell the truth."

"Sure enough," Amahl said, knowing now that he wasn't dreaming, "there are not two kings outside."

"That is surprising," replied his mother sarcastically.

Amahl tried to keep from grinning at her in triumph.

"The kings are three

and one of them is black."

Angry at last, his mother sat up.

"Oh! What shall I do with this boy!

If you were stronger, I'd like to whip you!"

"I knew it," Amahl murmured to himself.

His mother arose wearily from the bench. She pushed Amahl aside.

"I'm going to the door myself,

and then, young man,

you'll have to reckon with me!"

She went with determination toward the door and Amahl limped close behind her. As the door swung open and she saw the three kings standing there in all their splendor, she caught her breath. She bowed to them in utter amazement.

"Good evening," said the tall king with sweet blue eyes and a long white beard. "I am King Melchior." He wore rich robes trimmed with ermine, and silver slippers, and his voice was majestic but very kindly.

"Good evening," said a black king softly. "I am King Balthazar." He, too, was tall, but dark-bearded, and he wore robes of gold and scarlet and leopard skin.

"Good evening," said the third king. "I am Kaspar."

Amahl wanted to laugh with delight. Kaspar's robes, while they were rich, didn't fit him very well, and his crown was askew on his head as if he had just slapped it on any old way. His shoes didn't match, either—one was gold and the other was purple.

Amahl whispered triumphantly to his mother, "What did I tell you?"

"Noble sires," she said in an awed voice.

The black king, Balthazar, asked gently,
"May we rest a while in your house
and warm ourselves by your fireplace?"

Amahl's mother answered humbly,
"I am a poor widow.
A cold fireplace and a bed of straw
are all I have to offer you.
To these you are welcome."

King Kaspar, who seemed to be a little deaf, cupped his ear. "What did she say?"

Balthazar answered him. "That we are wel - come."

Kaspar smiled down at Amahl and his mother. Amahl clapped his hands with excitement. "Oh, thank you, thank you, thank you!" exclaimed Kaspar.

Then the three kings said together, "Thank you!"

"Come in, come in!" cried Amahl's mother. Still

bowing, she made way for the kings to enter her poor house, pulling Amahl with her.

As he watched, Amahl's eyes nearly popped out of his head. The page entered the cottage first. He placed his lantern on the low stool by the fireplace and put his bundles on the floor. Among the bundles were a rich Oriental rug and a golden cage holding a strange bird. Then the page hurried back to the door to carry King Kaspar's train.

Kaspar entered the room bearing an urn of incense and proceeded at a stately march in his ill-matched shoes across to the bench by the fireplace where he sat down. Balthazar, the sad, dark king, bearing a chalice of myrrh, entered next and strode over to sit on the bench beside Kaspar. The page scurried back to carry Melchior's train. Melchior was carrying a coffer of gold and Amahl noticed that he was wearing a ring with a ruby in it the size of a small egg. The coffer held more gold than Amahl and his mother had ever dreamed of in their lives.

Amahl rubbed his eyes. Then the page unrolled the rug and spread it before the kings and placed upon it the treasures they were carrying.

King Melchior looked around the bare clean room. "It's nice here," he said approvingly.

Amahl's mother, suddenly remembering that she was hostess to these marvelous guests, seized her shawl from the peg. Hurriedly she exclaimed,

"I shall go and gather wood for the fire.

I've nothing in the house."

Balthazar said. "We can only stay a little while. We must not lose sight of our star."

Amahl's mother paused. "Your star?"

Amahl whispered excitedly to his mother, "What did I tell you?"

"Sh!" said his mother, going toward the door.

Amahl's mother opened the door. "I shall be right back—and Amahl, don't be a nuisance." She went out quickly.

"No, Mother," said Amahl.

Kaspar arose from the bench and strode toward the corner of the fireplace where the page had placed the strange caged bird and a box covered with many-colored jewels and painted with mystic figures of dragons, bright-plumaged birds, and fantastic trees and flowers. Kaspar began to feed the strange bird bits of food from his pocket.

Amahl watched him a second, then hurried over to Balthazar and gazed up at him with admiration. He asked the black king,

"Are you a real king?

Have you regal blood?"

"Yes," answered Balthazar and his golden ear-
rings gleamed as he nodded his head. "I am a real
king."

"Can I see your regal blood?" asked Amahl.

"It is just like yours," answered Balthazar.

Amahl asked, "What's the use of having it, then?"

"No use," replied Balthazar.

Amahl asked eagerly, "Where is your home?"

Balthazar gazed sadly down at the boy and answered gently,

"I live in a black marble palace

full of black panthers and white doves.

And you, little boy,

what do you do?"

Amahl looked up at the king and told him sor-
rowfully,

"I was a shepherd. I had a flock of sheep,

but my mother sold them.

Now there are no sheep left.

I had a black goat who gave me warm sweet milk,

but she died of old age.

Now there is no goat left.

But Mother says that now

we shall both go begging from door to door.

Won't it be fun?"

Balthazar answered tersely, "It has its points."

Amahl crossed to the other side of the fireplace where Kaspar was still feeding his strange bird. "Are you a real king, too?" he asked.

Kaspar didn't answer and Amahl looked wonderingly back at Balthazar. Balthazar pointed to his own ear and shook his head, indicating that Kaspar was deaf. Amahl repeated his question in a shout.

"ARE YOU A REAL KING, TOO?"

This time Kaspar heard him. "Oh, truly, truly, truly, yes. I am a real king—am I not?" And he looked questioningly at Balthazar.

"Yes, Kaspar," Balthazar said.

Amahl giggled. He thought that Kaspar must surely be the funniest king in the world. He pointed at the caged bird. "What is that?"

"Eh?" asked Kaspar loudly.

Amahl shouted, "WHAT IS THAT?"

"A parrot," Kaspar replied.

Amahl had never seen such a strange bird. It had bright feathers and the cunning eyes of an old man. "Does it talk?" he inquired.

"Eh?" asked Kaspar and his tilted crown slid a little more to one side of his head.

"Does it talk?" Amahl repeated.

"How do I know?" Kaspar pointed to his deaf ear.

"Does it bite?" Amahl wanted to know.

"Eh?" asked Kaspar.

"DOES IT BITE?" Amahl shouted.

Kaspar held out a bandaged finger that Amahl hadn't noticed before. "Yes," said Kaspar.

Amahl pointed to the jeweled box painted with dragons and bright birds, unknown seas and strange trees and flowers. "And what is this?"

This time Kaspar heard him at once. With great excitement, the king opened the box, one drawer at a time, not allowing Amahl to see what he was going to take out next. Amahl marveled as Kaspar told him slowly,

"This is my box, this is my box,
I never travel without my box.
In the first drawer I keep my magic stones.
One carnelian against all evil and envy.
One moonstone to make you sleep.
One red coral to heal your wounds.
One lapis lazuli against quartan fever.
One small jasper to help you find water.

One small topaz to soothe your eyes.
One red ruby to protect you from lightning.
This is my box, this is my box,
I never travel without my box.
In the second drawer I keep all my beads.
Oh, how I love to play with beads—
all kinds of beads.
This is my box, this is my box,
I never travel without my box.
In the third drawer—
Oh, little boy! Oh, little boy!—
In the third drawer I keep
licorice—black, sweet licorice.
Have some."

Amahl had never seen licorice before but he
knew that it was candy. Now he *knew* that Kaspar
was the funniest king in the world. Although he
would have preferred bread, hungry as he was, he
seized a stick of the licorice and gobbled it down.
He swallowed the last morsel just as his mother opened
the door, returning with the few sticks of wood she
had been able to find.

Kaspar and Amahl jumped when she cried
sharply, "Amahl, I told you not to be a nuisance!"

Amahl hurried toward her. "But it isn't my

His hands are those of a king,
as king he was born.
But no one will bring him incense or gold,
though sick and poor and hungry and cold.
He's my child, my son,
my darling, my own."
The three kings looked at her, and then Melchior and Balthazar asked her together,
"Have you seen a Child
the color of earth, the color of thorn?
His eyes are sad,
His hands are those of the poor,
as poor He was born.
Incense, myrrh, and gold
we bring to His side,
and the eastern star is our guide."
Amahl's mother answered in a voice of grief,
"Yes, I know a child
the color of earth, the color of thorn.
His eyes are sad,
his hands are those of the poor,
as poor he was born.
But no one will bring him incense or gold,
though sick and poor and hungry and cold.
He's my child, my own."

fault!" he whispered discreetly. "They kept asking me questions."

His mother didn't believe him for one second. She commanded him firmly,

"I want you to go and call the other shepherds.
Tell them about our visitors,
and ask them to bring
whatever they have in the house,
as we have nothing to offer them.
Hurry on!"

"Yes, Mother," Amahl answered obediently. He grabbed up his cloak from his pallet, took his shepherd's hat from the peg and clapped it on his head. He tipped it sideways in imitation of King Kaspar's crown. He grinned at the three kings and at his mother and limped hastily out of the door. He certainly had wonderful news for the shepherds, and for once everybody would have to believe him.

When he had gone, his mother went toward the fireplace to set down the wood she had gathered. Then she saw once more, but this time near her feet, the coffer of gold, the urn of incense, and the chalice of myrrh, on the rich rug spread before the three kings. She dropped the wood and moved toward the treasures, holding out her thin hands.

She cried out in a voice of wonder,
"Oh, these beautiful things—
And all that gold!"
Melchior gazed at her with his blue eyes and
spoke softly. "These are the gifts to the Child."
"The child?" asked Amahl's mother. "Which
child?"
"We don't know," replied Melchior in a gentle
tone. "But the star will guide us to Him."
"But perhaps I know him," said Amahl's mother
eagerly. "What does he look like?"
Melchior gazed toward the window and asked
hopefully,
"Have you seen a Child
the color of wheat, the color of dawn?
His eyes are mild,
His hands are those of a King,
as King He was born.
Incense, myrrh, and gold
we bring to His side,
and the eastern star is our guide."
Amahl's mother answered as though to herself,
"Yes, I know a child
the color of wheat, the color of dawn.
His eyes are mild,

His hands are those of a king,
as king he was born.
But no one will bring him incense or gold,
though sick and poor and hungry and cold.
He's my child, my son,
my darling, my own."
The three kings looked at her, and then Melchior and Balthazar asked her together,
"Have you seen a Child
the color of earth, the color of thorn?
His eyes are sad,
His hands are those of the poor,
as poor He was born.
Incense, myrrh, and gold
we bring to His side,
and the eastern star is our guide."
Amahl's mother answered in a voice of grief,
"Yes, I know a child
the color of earth, the color of thorn.
His eyes are sad,
his hands are those of the poor,
as poor he was born.
But no one will bring him incense or gold,
though sick and poor and hungry and cold.
He's my child, my own."

Melchior stretched out his hand, the great ruby
burning on it before he turned it open.

"The Child we seek holds the seas
and the winds on His palm."

Kaspar swung his arm in a wide circle as he
said,

"The Child we seek has the moon
and the stars at His feet."

And Balthazar, the dark king, told Amahl's
mother,

"Before Him the eagle is gentle,
the lion is meek.
Choirs of angels hover over His roof
and sing Him to sleep.
He's warmed by breath,
He's fed by Mother
who is both Virgin and Queen.
Incense, myrrh, and gold
we bring to His side,
and the eastern star is our guide."

Amahl's mother walked slowly and with reluc-
tance away from the fireplace. She said in a low
voice, as if she were talking to herself,

"The child I know
on his palm holds my heart.

48

The child I know
at his feet has my life.
He's my child, my son,
my darling, my own,
and his name is Amahl."

The three kings fell silent, thinking of their quest, and Amahl's mother was silent, too, thinking of Amahl. The room was so quiet that Kaspar began to doze. But suddenly the call of the shepherds came sharp and clear through the winter air, breaking the hushed quiet of the room.

The shepherds signaled to one another, their voices echoing through the hills,

"Shepherds!"

"Who's calling?"

"Oh! Oh!"

Instinctively Amahl's mother glanced around to see if her home was ready to receive her neighbors. Then she went to the door and flung it wide. She told the kings proudly, "The shepherds are coming!"

Melchior nudged Kaspar, unwinding his golden shoe from his purple shoe. Kaspar sat up, blinked, and shook his head awake.

From the bench, the three kings gazed out of the doorway.

Lantern lights winked in and out of the hills. The shepherds began to appear from all directions, singly at first and then in small groups of two or three. The lights came flickering slowly down the road toward the cottage. Amahl limped ahead of the crowd, beckoning them on, his face radiant. The shepherds were calling to one another through the night.

"Emily, Emily,
Michael, Bartholomew,
how are your children and how are your sheep?
Dorothy, Dorothy,
Peter, Evangeline,
give me your hand, come along with me.
All the children have mumps.
All the flocks are asleep.
We are going with Amahl, bringing gifts to
    the kings.
Benjamin, Benjamin,
Lucas, Elizabeth,
how are your children and how are your sheep?
Carolyn, Carolyn,
Matthew, Veronica,
give me your hand, come along with me."
The three kings, sitting on the bench, watched

with pleasure as the shepherds, ragged and joyous, gathered in front of the cottage, bearing baskets of fruits and vegetables.

The shepherds shivered inside their cloaks and told each other,

"Brrr! How cold is the night!

Brrr! How icy is the wind!

Hold me very, very, very tight.

Oh, how warm is your cloak!

Katherine, Katherine,

Christopher, Babila,

how are your children and how are your sheep?

Josephine, Josephine,

Angela, Jeremy,

come along with me!"

The shepherds crowded together in the doorway and gasped to each other, "Look! Oh, look!" Amazed by the sight of the kings, they didn't dare to enter.

The kings smiled, and Amahl slipped through the people. He hurried to stand by his mother. And then, as she tried to coax the crowd in, Amahl felt proud of being the friend of kings, and he wanted to show off. He limped merrily across the room to stand beside the bench where the kings sat, and lifted his head haughtily. Now perhaps the children who had looked down on him for being a poor boy and a cripple would believe the dazzling sight before their eyes and show him proper respect! But he couldn't stay haughty long—he grinned in spite of himself.

His mother made a gesture of welcome toward her neighbors and urged them,

"Come in, come in!
What are you afraid of?
Don't be bashful, silly girl!
Don't be bashful, silly boy!
They won't eat you.
Show what you brought them."

Shy and embarrassed, each shepherd tried to push his neighbor in ahead of him. Finally all of them were crowded into one corner of the room and they gazed with awe at the gleaming gold and shining silver and glittering jewels and the bright-colored parrot in his cage. At length one shepherd gathered his courage and marched forward and laid his gifts before the kings. Then bowing shyly, he retreated hastily to his comrades.

The shepherds prodded each other,

"Go on, go on, go on!
No, you go on!"

Then they told the three kings,

"Olives and quinces, apples and raisins,
nutmeg and myrtle, medlars and chestnuts,
this is all we shepherds can offer you."
Kaspar, Melchior, and Balthazar answered graciously,
"Thank you, thank you,
thank you kindly."
A second shepherd crossed to the kings. He presented his gifts and bowed and returned to his friends. The kings told him,
"Thank you, thank you,
thank you kindly, too."
The shepherds said to the three kings,
"Citrons and lemons, musk and pomegranates,
goat cheese and walnuts, figs and cucumbers,
this is all we shepherds can offer you."
Kaspar, Melchior, and Balthazar answered,
"Thank you, thank you,
thank you kindly."
And as a third shepherd hastened forward with his gifts, they said,
"Thank you, thank you,
thank you kindly, too."
The shepherds told the kings,
"Hazelnuts and camomile, mignonette and laurel,

honeycombs and cinnamon, thyme, mint, and garlic,
this is all we shepherds can offer you."
The three kings replied gratefully,
"Thank you, thank you,
thank you kindly.
Thank you, thank you,
thank you kindly, too."
The shepherds cried to the kings,
"Take them, eat them,
you are welcome."
They said to the page,
"Take them, eat them,
you are welcome, too."
Amahl's mother beckoned to the young people.
"Now won't you dance for them?" she asked.

Amahl fetched his shepherd's pipe from the corner and went proudly to sit at the fireplace by an old bearded shepherd who already held his own pipe. Amahl smiled up at the old man and they both began to play the music for the dance. There was not a better piper than Amahl in all the hills, and he knew the gayest and quickest dances.

The shepherds called to each other,
"Don't be bashful, silly girl!

Don't be bashful, silly boy!
They won't eat you!"

The three kings watched with delight as a boy and a girl came shyly to the middle of the floor and began a dance to entertain the kings and show them welcome and hospitality. Gradually other dancers joined the first couple, and the music and the dance grew in pace and sureness. Amahl and the old shepherd piped faster and faster, till the dance ended in a joyous frenzy. Amahl and the old shepherd put down their pipes and smiled at each other, while the breathless dancers smiled and bowed to the kings.

Balthazar arose from the bench to thank the dancers.

"Thank you, good friends,
for your dances and your gifts.
But now we must bid you good night.
We have little time for sleep and a long journey ahead."
The shepherds replied,
"Good night, my good kings, good night and farewell.
The pale stones foretell that dawn is in sight.
Good night, my good kings, good night and farewell.

The night wind foretells that day will be bright."

The shepherds passed before the three kings, bowing as they departed. Amahl's mother said good night to them at the door and stood there for a moment, watching them go down the road. The lanterns twinkled among the hills and Amahl could hear their voices still calling, "Good night."

When Amahl's mother had closed the door, she said good night to the kings and prepared for herself a pallet of sheepskins on the floor. While she was busy, Amahl seized the opportunity to speak softly to Kaspar. He said, forgetting Kaspar's deafness,

"Excuse me, sir: Amongst your magic stones is there—is there one that could cure a cripple boy?"

Kaspar tried to straighten his crown as he looked down at him. "Eh?" he asked.

Defeated by Kaspar's deafness, Amahl went sadly to his pallet of straw. "Never mind," he told Kaspar and tried to smile at the funny worried king. "Good night." He lay down on his straw pallet, placing his crutch at his side. His thin cat crept out of the far corner where she had been hiding and snuggled into the crook of his arm again. Above his head his caged sparrow settled once more for sleep. "Oh, what's the use?" thought Amahl. His mother had tried all kinds of charms—the snakeskin, potions of herbs, wearing a curiously shaped stone tied around his neck—and nothing had worked. Amahl knew he was going to be a cripple for the rest of his life. He could hear the shepherds calling among the hills.

"Good night, good night,
The dawn is in sight.
Good night, farewell, good night."

Amahl yawned. He watched the three kings, still sitting on the rude bench, settle themselves for sleep, leaning against each other. Their servant curled himself up at their feet, his arms laid protectively over the rich gifts. He had placed his lantern on the floor by the fireplace, so that there was only a dim glow in the room. Amahl yawned again. He was determined not to go to sleep, for he wanted to see how kings looked when they slept. They looked very friendly, leaning against each other, as they shifted, attempting to get comfortable. But soon his eyes closed in spite of him.

Amahl's mother could not sleep. She sat on her pallet of sheepskins, thinking, and saw the first pale

rays of the dawn from the hills slowly enter the cottage. Her eyes kept returning to the treasure guarded by the page. She said to herself,

"All that gold! All that gold!
I wonder if rich people know what to do with their gold!
Do they know how a child could be fed?
Do rich people know?
Do they know that a house can be kept warm all day with burning logs?
Do rich people know?
Do they know how to roast sweet corn on a fire?
Do they know?
Do they know how to fill a courtyard with doves?
Do they?
Do they know how to milk a clover-fed goat?
Do they know how to spice hot wine on cold winter nights?
Do they know?
All that gold! All that gold!
Oh, what I could do for my child with that gold!
Why should it all go to a child they don't even know?
They are asleep. Do I dare?
If I take some they'll never miss it. . . ."

Slowly she drew herself across the floor, dragging her body with her hands. She told herself in a whisper,

"For my child—for my child—for my child. . . ."

But when she touched the gold, the page was instantly aroused. He sprang up and seized her arm, crying to his masters. Amahl's mother pulled frantically to free herself, dragging the page into the center of the room. But she still clutched the gold she had seized from Melchior's brimming coffer.

The page shouted at the top of his voice, "Thief! Thief!"

The kings awoke in confusion and stood up hastily. Melchior and Balthazar asked in startled voices, "What is it? What is it?"

The page shook her arm and shouted to the kings,

"I've seen her steal some of the gold!
She's a thief! Don't let her go!
She's stolen the gold!"

Melchior, Kaspar, and Balthazar said, "Shame! Shame!"

"Give it back!" yelled the page. "Or I'll tear it out of you!"

The noise awoke Amahl, who sat up completely

68

bewildered. But when he saw his mother being yanked about in the hands of the page, he struggled up with his crutch and awkwardly hurled himself upon the man. Kings or no kings, no one was going to hurt his mother! He beat the page hysterically and pulled his hair, in an effort to force the man to release her.

The kings and the page cried, "Give the gold back! Give it back!"

Amahl yelled in a fury, hitting the page, "Don't you dare!

Don't you dare, ugly man, hurt my mother!

I'll smash in your face!

I'll knock out your teeth!

Don't you dare!

Don't you dare, ugly man, hurt my mother!"

He rushed to King Kaspar and tugged at his robe.

"Oh, Mister King, don't let him hurt my mother!

My mother is good.

She cannot do anything wrong.

I'm the one who lies. I'm the one who steals."

He hobbled frantically back to attack the page again and shouted,

"Don't you dare!

70

Don't you dare, ugly man, hurt my mother!
I'll break all your bones!
I'll bash in your head!"

At a sign from Kaspar, the page let go of Amahl's mother's arm. Kneeling on the floor, she lifted her arms toward Amahl. Choked by tears, Amahl staggered toward her, and letting his crutch fall, collapsed, sobbing, into his mother's arms.

Melchior looked at the boy and his mother with compassion and said gently,

"Oh, woman, you may keep the gold.
The Child we seek doesn't need our gold.
On love, on love alone
He will build His kingdom.
His pierced hand will hold no scepter,
His haloed head will wear no crown.
His might will not be built on your toil.
Swifter than lightning
He will soon walk among us.
He will bring us new life and receive our death,
and the keys to His city belong to the poor."

Melchior turned to Balthazar and Kaspar and said to them, "Let us leave, my friends."

Freeing herself from Amahl's embrace, his

mother threw herself on her knees before the kings. She spilled onto the rug the gold she had taken. Amahl got to his feet, leaning on his crutch, his face still wet with tears.

His mother said, sobbing, to the three kings, "Oh, no, wait—take back your gold!
For such a King I've waited all my life,
And if I weren't so poor
I would send a gift of my own to such a Child."

Amahl limped forward eagerly and said, "Yes, let's send Him a gift."

But his mother asked, "What can we send? We are so poor."

Amahl suddenly had an idea. Perhaps this Child was as lonely as he had been and his heart went out to him. What if the Child were a cripple like himself? He looked at the kings and then back at his mother.

"Mother," he exclaimed, "let me send Him my crutch.
Who knows, He may need one,
and this I made myself."

His mother protested, "But that you can't, you can't! How could you get about without it?"

73

She hurried to stop him as he lifted the worn crutch.

Amahl took one step toward the kings, then realized that he had moved without the help of his crutch. Astounded, he whispered, "I walk, Mother! I walk, Mother!"

His leg that had felt like a dead branch on a tree suddenly felt warm and strong. He felt the blood rushing through it and it ached, but it was a glorious ache. Amahl took another step, then another, then tried a little dance turn and skip toward the three kings.

Kaspar, Melchior, Balthazar, and his mother exulted together in awe,

"He walks! He walks! He walks! He walks!"

Step by step, Amahl made his way toward the kings, holding his crutch before him in his outstretched hands. His mother stood back, almost fearful of the miracle she was beholding.

Kaspar, Melchior, and Balthazar marveled together,

"It is a sign from the Holy Child.
We must give praise to the newborn King.
We must praise Him.
This is a sign from God!"

Amahl placed the crutch in the waiting hands of Kaspar and walked uncertainly to the center of the room. He began to grow confident and joy leaped in his legs. His crippled leg grew stronger by the minute. He jumped over his pallet and scared his thin cat, and his caged sparrow set up a frightened chirping, answered by a loud squawk from Kaspar's parrot. He ran toward his mother and then away from her, and shouted,

"Look, Mother! I can dance,
I can jump, I can run!"

Kaspar, Melchior, and Balthazar exclaimed in wonder,

"Truly, he can dance,
he can jump, he can run!"

Amahl flung open the door and dashed madly in and out of the house, then round and round the room. His mother and the three kings, afraid he would fall, chased after him, but Amahl was too quick, and they could not catch him. Afraid he would fall! Amahl laughed with delight and nearly knocked Kaspar over. Delirious, he kept on prancing until finally he turned a clumsy pirouette. Then he did stumble and fall to the floor. He was chagrined and angry at himself. Why did he always overdo things?

His mother went to him quickly and lifted him from the floor.

"Please, my darling, be careful now.

You must take care not to hurt yourself."

The three kings, breathless, told his mother,

"Oh, good woman, you must not be afraid.

For he is loved by the Son of God."

Amahl stood, supported by his mother, while each of the three kings asked, "Oh, blessed child, may I touch you?" One at a time, the kings passed before Amahl and laid their hands upon his hair. Amahl moved slightly away from his mother and stood alone, watching the page come across the room.

The page prostrated himself before Amahl and asked, "Oh, blessed child, may I touch you?"

Amahl had not forgotten that it was the page who had seized his mother and yanked her arm. Then he had been only a poor cripple boy unable to defend her. Now they all wanted to win his good graces. He frowned. He felt suddenly self-important and enjoyed it. He told the page, "Well, I don't know if I'm going to let *you* touch me."

"Amahl!" his mother said in gentle reproof.

"Oh, all right—but just once," said Amahl.

When the page had touched his hand briefly, he

laughed and did a gay little dance step. He pleaded,
"Look, Mother, I can fight,
I can work, I can play!
Oh, Mother, let me go with the kings!
I want to take the crutch to the Child myself."

Kaspar, Melchior, and Balthazar, struck by the idea, added their plea to Amahl's.

"Yes, good woman, let him come with us!
We'll take good care of him,
We'll bring him back on a camel's back."

Amahl's mother, her heart in her eyes, knelt before him. "Do you really want to go?" she asked.

Amahl was very excited at the thought of seeing the Child for whom the kings were seeking, the Child who had made him walk. Then, too, there was the adventure of seeing something of the world, for he had never been beyond the hills around him where he had been born. And the kings had said they would bring him back on a camel. What would the other shepherd boys think when he came riding home on a camel?

All of it would be wonderful!

"Yes, Mother," he answered eagerly.

His mother insisted, "Are you sure, sure, sure?"

"I'm sure!" cried Amahl.

His mother astonished him. She agreed with him.

"Yes, I think you should go,
and bring thanks to the Child yourself."

Amahl couldn't quite believe his ears. He asked, "Are you sure, sure, sure?"

"Go on, get ready," his mother told him.

Kaspar asked, "What did she say?"

Balthazar answered solemnly, "She said he can come."

"Oh, lovely, lovely!" cried Kaspar. "We can play marbles together with my precious stones, and I'll share my licorice with him!"

Amahl thought Kaspar was the most wonderful king he would ever see, as well as the funniest. His mother bustled about, packing his few poor homespun clothes into a bundle. "What to do with your crutch?" she asked.

"You can tie it to my back," answered Amahl, picking up his shepherd's pipe.

"Don't forget your hat!" his mother said anxiously.

Amahl promised her, "I shall always wear my hat." He wished she wouldn't worry so much.

She said bravely, "So, my darling, good-by!"

Amahl felt like weeping and shouting with joy to the stars at the same time. He and his mother both said together,

"So, my darling, good-by!
I shall miss you very much."

Of course, his mother had to start fussing. "Wash your ears!" she said.

"Yes, I promise," said Amahl.

"Don't tell lies!" warned his mother.

"No, I promise." And this time Amahl knew he would never lie again. He had some things to ask of his mother. "Feed my bird!"

"Yes, I promise," his mother said.

"Watch the cat!"

"Yes, I promise."

"I shall miss you very much," said Amahl, swallowing.

The kings had been gathering up their gifts to the Child, making ready for the departure. Off in the hills, the shepherds called to one another as they began the chores of the new day.

Melchior looked down at Amahl out of his blue

eyes and his white beard moved up and down as he spoke. "Are you ready?"

"Yes, I'm ready," Amahl answered, feeling very small.

"Let's go, then," said Melchior briskly.

The page picked up his burdens and the heavy lantern. The three kings started their stately procession out of the cottage, bowing their thanks to Amahl's mother as they went. In the blue snow-frosted hills, the shepherds called,

"Come, O shepherds, come outside.

All the stars have left the sky.

O sweet dawn—O, dawn of peace!"

Amahl rushed into his mother's arms, hugged her, and kissed her good-by. The page was untying the camels from the fig trees outside and the camels stamped in the road. Amahl gave his mother a final hug and rushed out of the house, his pipe in his hand, calling, "Wait for me!"

Melchior and Balthazar were already seated on their camels. Kaspar, his one gold shoe and his one purple shoe kicking up the dust of the road, lifted Amahl to the front of the seat on his own camel.

"Eh? Hold onto the parrot until I get up!" Kaspar said. "And then I'll hold onto both of you."

Amahl held on to the caged parrot who gave him a cunning sidewise glance and said, "Awk."

Amahl laughed.

"Ha, ha, ha!" mimicked the parrot.

Kaspar, helped by the page, settled himself on the camel behind Amahl and put his arms around him and the parrot cage as he took up the silver reins and clucked the camel forward after Melchior and Balthazar.

Amahl squirmed around. His mother was standing lonely in the doorway of their cottage. He waved at her violently and she waved back. Then he saw her come outside of the cottage. He and Kaspar and the parrot nearly fell off the camel as he waved for the last time. A bend in the road shut the cottage from his sight.

Amahl leaned back against Kaspar's chest, then lifted his pipe and began to play. The soft colors of dawn were brightening the sky, and Amahl saw the shepherds stop tending their flocks to listen to him. As the camels swayed onward, he piped all the songs he knew for the kings and for his shepherd neighbors, but he was certain that now he was also playing for the new Christ Child.

Melchior and Balthazar, Kaspar and Amahl, the sleeping parrot and the camels, moved slowly onward toward the great star.